1: The Arduous Business of Getting Rescued

JAN 18

MUST *WRITE.*

MUST NOT GO *STUPID.*

...very far. ...at night when no one else is around. Sparky and I have a... ...at the hands of... ...beginning to question whether getting rescued is... The worst thing that could happen to me. Sure, the princes that ha... ...tried so far have all been pompous and, apparently, tasty, but that doesn't mean that there isn't a guy out there for me somewhere. Right? I should have known better than to trust my parents. You know how they got me here? **Poison!** On my sixteenth birthday, after weeks of fighting about whether I, like my five older sisters before me, should be locked away to be some prince's trophy, my mother finally conceded. "You know what Adrienne dear," she asked, "Your father and I have finally decided that you are right. You are too intelligent and self—reliant to be won by some old prince." Then, for my birthday dinner, she had ...ooks make my... ...meal. I was elbows deep in steak before I realized ...lif... ...**BOOM,** I wake up in a tower.

STUPID PARENTS.

UM, *HELLO?*

WHAT *NOW?*

DEAD.

SOMEONE IS GOING TO *PAY* FOR THIS!

PUT THE WORD OUT THROUGH *ALL* SEVEN REGIONS OF THE KINGDOM.

I WANT THE GREATEST KNIGHTS IN ALL THE LAND HERE *TOMORROW!*

I *WANT* THAT DRAGON'S HEAD ON MY MANTLE BY WEEK'S END.

IT WILL SERVE AS A *WARNING* OF WHAT HAPPENS TO THOSE WHO DARE DEFY ME!

FWOOOM

WHOA!

WHAT!

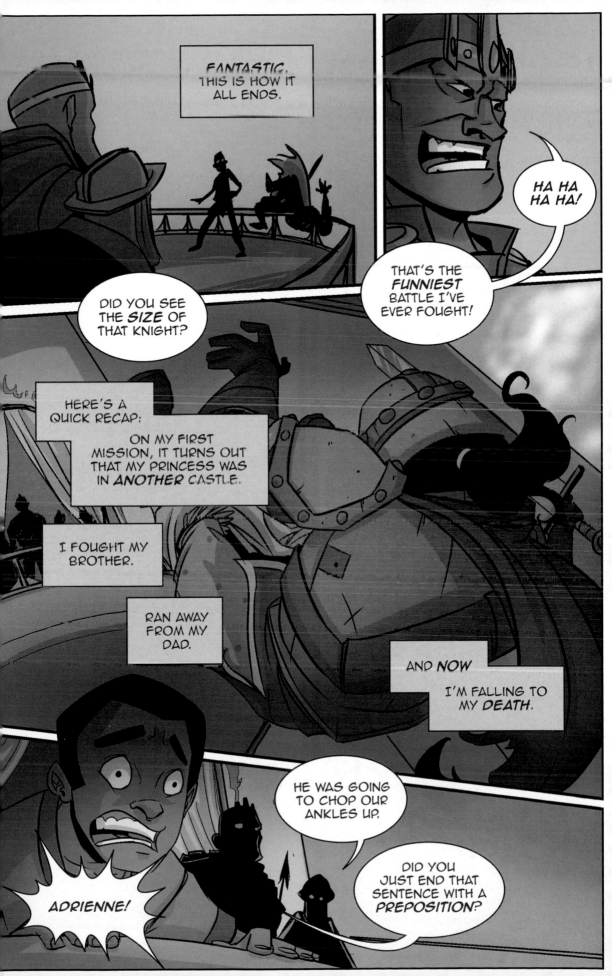

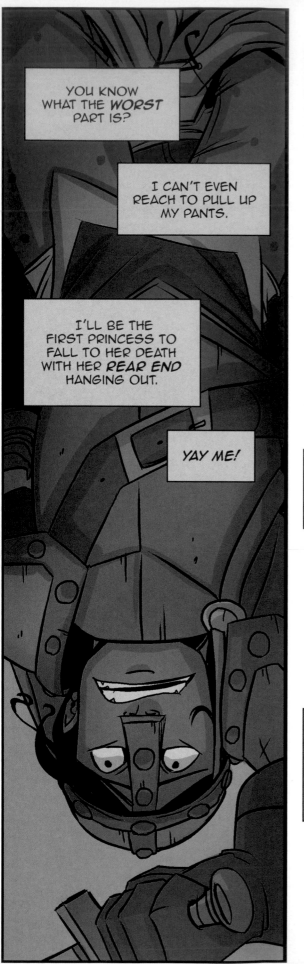

YOU KNOW WHAT THE *WORST* PART IS?

I CAN'T EVEN REACH TO PULL UP MY PANTS.

I'LL BE THE FIRST PRINCESS TO FALL TO HER DEATH WITH HER *REAR END* HANGING OUT.

YAY ME!

THEY'LL HAVE TO CALL MY MOM IN JUST TO IDENTIFY ME.

YES, THAT'S THE TOOSHIE THAT I WIPED AND SPANKED FOR ALL THOSE YEARS. I'D RECOGNIZE IT *ANYWHERE*.

WHY DID OUR CASTLE HAVE TO BE SO *TALL?*

THIS IS TAKING *FOREVER!*

I DECIDE TO FORGET ABOUT THAT, JUST CLOSE MY EYES, AND WAIT FOR THE *SPLAT*

WORST HEROINE *EVER.*

3: On Sexism in the Armor Industry

THAT EXPLAINS A *LOT!*

I *THOUGHT* I SAW *POLKA DOTS* WHEN YOU FELL THROUGH THE ROOF.

WOULDN'T BE THE STRANGEST THING I'VE SEEN FROM A KNIGHT.

YOU PROBABLY WON'T SELL ARMOR TO A GIRL, HUH?

AU CONTRAIRE, COME WITH ME.

Y'KNOW, YOU LOOK AWFULLY FAMILIAR. HAVE I SEEN YOU SOMEWHERE?

NOT LIKELY, I DON'T GET OUT MUCH.

ALL EVIDENCE TO THE CONTRARY.

BEHOLD, THE *WOMEN WARRIORS* COLLECTION!

THERE ARE *WOMEN WARRIORS?*

MORE THAN YOU'D THINK. THIS IS ONE OF THE MOST POPULAR... AT LEAST AMONG *FANS* OF WOMEN WARRIORS.

THE CHAIN MAIL BRA HAS A SUPER INDUSTRIAL CLASP TO MAKE SURE YOUR BOSOMS STAY SECURE IN THE HEAT OF BATTLE.

WOW.

WE CALL IT "THE SONYA".

WOULDN'T *THAT* GIVE YOU A WEDGIE?

THE SHORT ANSWER? *YES.*

THE LONG ANSWER IS ALSO YES, BUT THAT'S THE LEAST PAINFUL THING IT DOES.

BUT WHAT'S MORE IMPORTANT, COMFORT OR LOOKING GOOD?

MOVING ON. THIS IS "THE DIANA".

IT COMES WITH A METAL BREAST PLATE, CLOTH SHIRT, AND MINI-TIGHTS.

THE TIGHTS COME WITH OR WITHOUT LIMITED METAL PLATING. OH, AND THESE DARLING BANGLES.

SO, IF THE CHEST IS PLATED WITH ARMOR, WHY NOT THE REST OF IT?

I DON'T UNDERSTAND.

WHAT IF SOMEONE TRIES TO STAB ME IN THE STOMACH?

THAT'S WHAT THE BRACELETS ARE FOR-- TO DEFLECT WEAPONS.

BUT WHAT IF SOMEONE TRIES TO STAB ME WHILE I'M TRYING TO STAB THEM?

OH, THERE'S NO SWORD WITH THIS ONE... JUST A ROPE.

YOU'RE THE...

YOU'RE PRINCESS ADRIENNE!

DO YOU KNOW WHO YOU ARE?

OH MY GOD! THE PRINCESS WANTS TO BUY SOME OF MY ARMOR.

THE PRINCESS IS GOING TO WEAR SOMETHING I MADE!

SOMETHING YOU MADE?

YOU MADE ALL THIS ARMOR?

OOPS.

PLEASE DON'T TELL ANYONE! MY DAD HASN'T MADE ARMOR IN YEARS.

HE SPENDS ALL HIS TIME AT THE PUB. IF I HADN'T LEARNED HOW TO SMITH, WE'D BE OUT IN THE STREET BY NOW.

IF ANYONE FINDS OUT THAT SOME TEENAGE GIRL IS MAKING THE ARMOR, THEY'LL NEVER BUY ANYTHING.

SO, YOU DESIGNED ALL THESE SKIMPY COSTUMES FOR "WOMEN WARRIORS"?

YES.

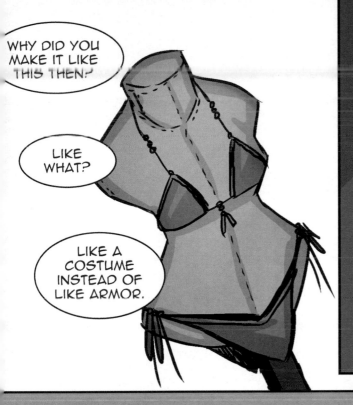

WHY DID YOU MAKE IT LIKE THIS THEN?

LIKE WHAT?

LIKE A COSTUME INSTEAD OF LIKE ARMOR.

IT *IS* ARMOR.

WHAT I'M SAYING IS WHY SHOULD A WOMAN'S ARMOR HAVE TO SHOW CLEAVAGE? OR STOMACH?

SO...WAIT... *WHAT?*

OKAY, LET'S TRY THIS AGAIN.

WHY NOT MAKE REAL ARMOR, WHICH WOULD ACTUALLY BE EFFECTIVE IN A FIGHT, FOR A WOMAN WARRIOR?

FWOOSH!

PUH!

I GUESS I'LL WAIT HERE THEN.

THUMP!

UMMM... DO YOU MIND TELLING ME WHAT'S GOING ON?

ISN'T IT OBVIOUS? THEY'RE TRYING TO KILL ME!

SWIIIISH

YEAH, BUT WHY? YOU'RE THE PRI--

I DIDN'T ASK, BEDELIA.

IT MIGHT BE BECAUSE THEY THINK I KILLED A PRINCESS AND TRIED TO KILL ANOTHER ONE.

BUT YOU *ARE* THE PR--

I KNOW THAT, BUT THEY *DON'T*, SO QUIT SAYING IT! *GAH!*

IS THERE ANOTHER WAY OUT OF HERE? A BACK DOOR OR SOMETHING?

UH...NO, THERE'S A BALCONY UPSTAIRS BUT THAT GOES RIGHT OUT ONTO THE STREET.

WELL, THERE'S ONE DOOR, BUT IT JUST GOES TO THE NEXT STORE OVER, WHICH PUTS YOU ON THE STREET.

THEY'RE PROBABLY IN THERE ALREADY TOO. WE NEED A PLAN.

WE'VE GOT PLENTY OF TIME!

MY DAD BUILT THAT DOOR, THERE'S NO WAY THEY'LL BREAK IT IN.

DO YOU SMELL THAT?

IT'S A *BLACKSMITH*. IT ALWAYS SMELLS LIKE THAT IN HERE.

LIKE WHAT?

OH, LIKE FIRE.

WELL, THAT AIN'T GOOD.

QUICK, GET ON THE FLOOR. I READ THAT YOU CAN BREATH BETTER DOWN THERE.

OOH, THAT'S NEAT. I'LL HAVE TO REMEMBER THAT THE *NEXT TIME* I SET THE SHOP ON FIRE.

DOES THAT HAPPEN MUCH?

JUST ONCE... OR MAYBE TWICE... DOES IT COUNT IF I SET SOMEBODY ELSE'S SHOP ON FIRE?

YOU KNOW, THIS WOULD BE A LOT WORSE IF MOST OF THE SMOKE WASN'T GOING THROUGH THE PRINCESS SHAPED HOLE IN THE ROOF.

I THINK WE SHOULD GO UPSTAIRS.

THAT OUGHTA TEACH 'EM!

YEAH, THESE WOMEN GOTTA LEARN THEIR *PLACE*.

SO... I FORGOT, WHY WERE WE HARASSING PEOPLE IN TOWN TODAY?

I THINK WE WERE LOOKING FOR SOMEONE. WAS IT A KNIGHT?

OH YEAH, WE WERE LOOKING FOR THAT SHORT KNIGHT WITH THE DRAGON.

FAR AS I'M CONCERNED HE DON'T NEVER NEED TO HEAR WE'RE THE ONES STARTED THIS FIRE. SEEMS A PERFECT FIT FOR A DRAGON, EH?

YOU DON'T SUPPOSE THE KING'LL BE MAD WHEN HE FINDS OUT THAT INSTEAD OF FINDING THIS KNIGHT WE ENDED UP BURNING DOWN THE BLACKSMITH?

TOO RIGHT! AND THE BLACKSMITH'S A *DWARF*. WHO'S GOING TO LISTEN TO THE WORD OF A DWARF OVER THE KING'S MEN?

NOBODY, THAT'S WHO.

ALL WE HAVE TO DO IS GET BACK TO THE CASTLE WITH- OUT GETTING IN ANY MORE SCRAPES.

!

SLURP!

HRRRRM!

AWW, SHE LIKES YOU!

HUH...HUH... HER TONGUE IS SO WARM. I DIDN'T EXPECT IT TO BE SO WARM.

GOOD DRAGON... PLEASE DON'T EAT ME... GOOD DRAGON.

THIS MAN, THIS DWARF, HE CAME TO THE KING TO COMPLAIN THAT HIS SHOP HAD BEEN BURNT DOWN AND HIS DAUGHTER KILLED.

OH MY...

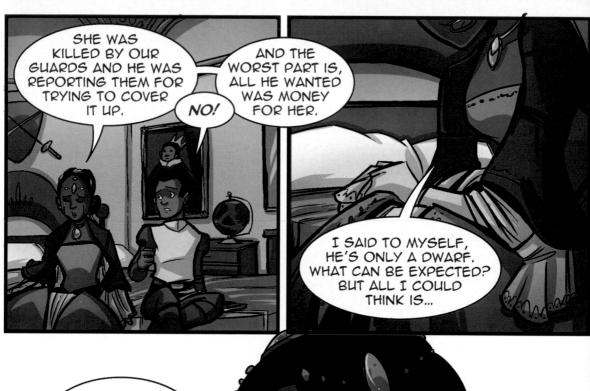

SHE WAS KILLED BY OUR GUARDS AND HE WAS REPORTING THEM FOR TRYING TO COVER IT UP.

NO!

AND THE WORST PART IS, ALL HE WANTED WAS MONEY FOR HER.

I SAID TO MYSELF, HE'S ONLY A DWARF. WHAT CAN BE EXPECTED? BUT ALL I COULD THINK IS...

...THAT'S EXACTLY HOW I'VE ACTED ABOUT ADRIENNE.

MOTHER, DON'T DO THIS TO YOURSELF.

MY DAUGHTER IS DEAD AND I HAVEN'T EVEN THOUGHT TO BE SAD, JUST *ANGRY*.

MOTHER...

...I HAVE TO TELL YOU SOMETHING...

AND *NOW* WHAT YOU'VE ALL BEEN *WAITING FOR...*

OKAY SPARKY, SETTLE IN BEHIND SOME TREES AND STAY OUT OF SIGHT.

WE'VE GOT TO RESUPPLY BEFORE THE NEXT PART OF OUR QUEST.

SHOPPE

I USED TO BE AN ADVENTURER LIKE YOU, THEN I TOOK AN ARROW IN THE KNEE...

YER *KIDDIN'*, RIGHT?

I BEEN STUCK WITH *DOZENS* O'ARROWS, BOLTS, SPEARS AN' POINTED *STICKS!*

ADMIT IT!

YE STOPPED ADVENTURIN' 'CAUSE YOU WENT ALL *WIMPY-HEADED!*

IF I GAVE UP 'CAUSE I GOT *NICKED* BY A WEE SPLINT SHAFT,

TH' DWARVEN GODS'D HAMMER MAH SOUL INTO *ARMORED UNDERPANTS!*

DRY
RATIONS

DRY & ASTELESS TIONS

RATIONS
-DRY-
(MAY CONTAIN WOOD CHIPS)

WOO CHIP YUM

END

SKULLKICKERS IS PUBLISHED BY IMAGE COMICS.

PIN-UP BY TRESSA BOWLING

Princeless!

M Moriarty 2012

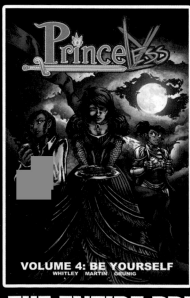

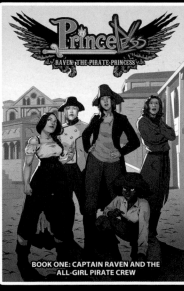